The Pirate Veggies!

BANTAM BOOKS

Hello there, Tiddlers!

I'm Mr Bloom, welcome to my nursery.

I've just been digging up potatoes. It's amazing what you find underground!

Now, shall I tell you a story? I've got just the one! It's about the time the Veggies set sail on the high seas, in search of something super-sparkly . . .

One day, I came into the nursery to find Raymond covered in blue, sparkly glitter. It was all over him! I asked what had happened to make such a mess.

"I've been telling Margaret all about pirates, with their maps and their hats," Raymond explained to me. "And how they like to go sailing on the blue, sparkly sea!"

"Then I decided to paint a picture of the blue, sparkly sea," Margaret said. "My picture shows some fish and lots of other sea creatures. But it isn't sparkly!" she sighed.

Raymond had wanted to help Margaret finish her picture, so he decided to find some sparkly glitter. He looked all around the nursery until he spotted just what he needed.

The jar of sparkly glitter was up on a high shelf. But when Raymond reached up to get it, he knocked the jar and it fell . . . And landed on top of him, covering him in blue sparkles!

"Oh no, that was the last jar of sparkly glitter! How will I finish my picture now?" Margaret wailed.

"I'm so sorry, Margaret," Raymond said sadly.

Suddenly, Compo's fans began to **whirr** and his pistons started to **chug**. Then there was the **clank clank clank** of levers and he began to blow bubbles, which floated across the nursery.

"Oh, I wonder what Compo has for us? Perhaps it's some more sparkly glitter!" Raymond hoped.

But instead, one of Compo's drawers opened to reveal a piece of paper with a strange drawing on.

"Look, Veggies, it's a treasure map, just like pirates have!" I said, taking out the paper and holding it up for them all to see.

The Veggies were very excited.

"Then we must become pirates and follow the map to find the treasure," Margaret decided straight away. "Thank you, Compo!"

"Pirate Bean!" Colin cried.

"But we can't be pirates looking like this. We'll need some costumes!" Margaret said.

"Good idea, Margaret," I replied, turning back to Compo. Perhaps he could help!

Again, Compo's fans **whirred**, his pistons **chugged** and his levers **clanked**. This time when the drawer popped open, little black pirate hats were inside.

"They're your size, Veggies!" I said, putting the hats on Margaret, Raymond and Colin.

"We need a boat if we're going to be pirates," Raymond said.

"Don't worry, Raymond, I've got just the thing!" I told him, before heading out into my allotment for a moment.

I quickly returned with their old wheelbarrow pram, which I'd made into a pirate ship. It even had a sail!

"Now you're ready," I said, placing Margaret, Raymond and Colin safely inside the ship.

"So, where does the map say to go?" I asked the Veggies, laying the map out in front of them.

"That's our Veggie patch and that's Compo. It's a map of the nursery!" Margaret soon realised.

"Then let's sail over yonder! Oh arrr!" I replied in my best pirate voice.

Following Compo's map, I wheeled them around plant pots and between boxes of seeds until . . .

X marks the spot!

"We're here!" Raymond cried, standing right in the middle of the sandpit. "The treasure must be underground!"

"Digging Bean!" Colin said, keen to get started.

So the Veggies watched as I began to dig, shovelling the sand out of the way.

"A treasure chest!" Margaret gasped as it was finally uncovered.

Can you guess what was inside it, Tiddlers?

"Sparkly glitter! Now you can finish your picture, Margaret!" Raymond chuckled when I lifted the lid and took out the treasure.

"Yes, my sea will be all lovely and sparkly now," Margaret smiled.

So, finally Margaret's picture of the sea was both blue *and* sparkly! How about that, Tiddlers?

Now it's time for me and the Veggies to say goodbye. We've had lots of fun today, and we'll see you again very soon!

MR BLOOM'S NURSERY: THE PIRATE VEGGIES!
A BANTAM BOOK 978 0 857 51247 5

Published in Great Britain by Bantam,
an imprint of Random House Children's Publishers UK
A Random House Group Company.

This edition published 2013

1 3 5 7 9 10 8 6 4 2

Bantam Books are published by Random House Children's Publishers UK,
61–63 Uxbridge Road, London W5 5SA

www.**randomhousechildrens**.co.uk

Addresses for companies within The Random House Group Limited can be found at:
www.randomhouse.co.uk/offices.htm

THE RANDOM HOUSE GROUP Limited Reg. No. 954009

A CIP catalogue record for this book is available from the British Library

Printed in China

The Random House Group Limited supports The Forest Stewardship Council (FSC®),
the leading international forest certification organization. Our books carrying the FSC label are
printed on FSC®-certified paper. FSC is the only forest certification scheme endorsed by the leading
environmental organizations, including Greenpeace. Our paper procurement policy can be found at
www.randomhouse.co.uk/environment

MIX
Paper from
responsible sources
FSC® C020056